To Dylan, for reaching out to a shy kid.
To Chris, for your friendship and all your help along the way.
—Nicholas

To my kids, who are filling my life with the colors of happiness!
—Renia

Text Copyright © 2021 Nicholas Solis
Illustration Copyright © 2021 Renia Metallinou
Design © 2021 Sleeping Bear Press

 SLEEPING BEAR PRESS™

2395 South Huron Parkway, Suite 200
Ann Arbor, MI 48104
www.sleepingbearpress.com
© Sleeping Bear Press

Printed and bound in China.
10 9 8 7 6 5 4 3 2 1

ISBN: 978-1-53411-105-9

Library of Congress Cataloging-in-Publication Data
Names: Solis, Nicholas, author. | Metallinou, Renia, illustrator.
Title: The color collector / by Nicholas Solis ; illustrated by Renia Metallinou.
Description: Ann Arbor, MI : Sleeping Bear Press, [2021] | Audience: Ages 6-10. |
Summary: "When a boy notices the new girl collecting litter on their walks home, he wants to
know why. She shows him the mural she's created that reminds her of the home she left behind.
They both find how wonderful it is to make a new friend"— Provided by publisher.
Identifiers: LCCN 2020039897 | ISBN 9781534111059 (hardcover) Subjects: CYAC: Friendship—Fiction. |
Immigrants—Fiction. | Homesickness—Fiction. | Art—Fiction. Classification: LCC PZ7.1.S668 Co 2021 |
DDC [E]—dc23 | LC record available at https://lccn.loc.gov/2020039897

The Color Collector

By Nicholas Solis

Illustrated by
RENIA METALLINOU

PUBLISHED BY SLEEPING BEAR PRESS™

She was new.
She was quiet.
I think she was lonely.

That was the day I met Violet.

I was new once.
I said hello.

She smiled a little, I think.
But she was quiet.

She lived near me.
We walked home the same way.
I was on one side, she on the other.

Always quiet.

Always alone.

Every day the same.

Until one day.

The day she picked something up.

The wind blew strong.
A **red** candy wrapper did somersaults.

It landed at her feet. It hugged her shoe.

Violet picked it up.
The bright red wrapper.

Then it was gone.
Disappearing into her backpack.

She looked up.
She looked at me.
She waved.

Then her eyes went down
and she turned the corner.

She was always picking things up.
I had never noticed it before.
Now it is all I see her do.

Bright **blue** cookie wrappers.

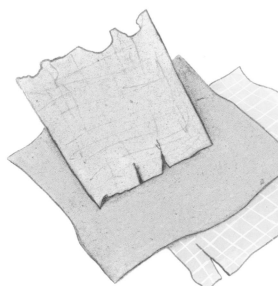

Yellow pieces of paper.

Green bottle caps.

Red fall leaves.

All disappearing
into the **gray** backpack.

One day, on our silent walk home,
I am not so silent.

"What do you do with it all?"

"All of what?"

"The wrappers and
trash and leaves."

"Do you really want to know?"

"Yes, please."

"Then follow me."

"Just a little farther."

Up one flight of stairs.

Then another.

And another.

The heavy door creaks open.
"This is my room."

Here, in her room, the sun comes to shine.
It reaches in and makes her glow.
It makes her collection glow as well.

Each brightly colored wrapper,
piece of trash, and speckled leaf
has a place on her walls, her ceiling, her door.
They are no longer forgotten bits blowing in the wind.
Along her wall they are one.

They are her sky,

her beach,

her village.

They are beautiful.

"We came here for a better life. I miss home, though.
I miss the sounds and smells. And I miss the colors."

I am sad that she is sad. "It is beautiful," I say.

She tells me stories . . .
about her sun,
her ocean,
her people.

We sit
and talk.

Then laugh.

Then talk
some more.

She is not so sad.
She is not so alone.
It feels good to be her friend.

I say goodbye.

She says goodbye.

"I'll see you tomorrow."

It is true.

She smiles.

I smile.

We smile the same.

On my way home.
The wind blows strong and cold.

A bright red leaf
falls at my feet.

I pick it up and
put it in my backpack.